Once Upon a Time We Were Free

By John Rotondo

Contents

Once upon a time we were free

Preface

This story takes a reflective look at a day in the life of a salesman. You will note that he has no name; he is anonymous. The events take place at a future time in the novel's present day, but also refers back to the past. This future time line is intentionally distorted and is an alternate reality (we hope) as he valiantly tries to cling to the values that he holds dear. This is also depicted in defiant tics he uses to expel his frustrations. The story compares values of today (the current day) against the values of the past and again to what might be those of the future. It is a constant battle to resist change and adjust where one has to.

A number of social issues of our present day are expanded into this alternate future. Note that the basic idea of laws and rules discussed are those that take place in some form in our own present time.

Although just a salesman, this person has quite an interesting past and future. Before being a salesman he was quite important to the government and on a number of occasions he did more than his part to make a difference.

There are no direct real life people in the story; it is fiction. The characters depicted are a composition of individuals encountered through the author's experiences and also contrived where necessary.

The present time of the book, our alternate future, will not definitely happen, but can happen if we let it.

Read through and enjoy. Decide for yourself what you feel is real, right and politically correct behavior. Never let any one, this author included, impose what they feel is correct upon you. This is ultimately a decision YOU have to make.

About the Author
John Rotondo

John Rotondo is currently the President of Saturn 5, Inc., an innovation company that develops and promotes ideas for new products. Mr. Rotondo received his degree in computer systems design in 1992. Additionally, he attended classes in pursuit of mechanical and chemical engineering degrees.

He has worked in the aerospace industry and also the apparel industry, his current profession.

Mr. Rotondo attended school while serving as Vice President of a multi-state real estate property management company.

Mr. Rotondo was one of the original founders of this company in 1982. He served as Vice President of the corporation and the computer systems department while managing a portfolio of clients. From 1994 to 2006 he became president of the corporation.

In 2006, Mr. Rotondo sold his interest in that business in order to pursue his other interests.

In 2010, Mr. Rotondo received a provisional U.S. utility patent # 61/353,852 for a new type of lens. This lens transfers light proportionally from one location to a target. The term coined for this process is light transposition.

In 2005, Mr. Rotondo received a utility patent US 6,845,918 B2 for one of his designs. This electronic device controls and causes a common air-conditioner to be more reactive to the environment it is cooling.

Chapter 1

- - -

Today (tomorrow)

I'm gazing out the window awaiting my ride to approach and I'm a little anxious because as usual we are running a little late. I need to catch the 8:05 train into the city. It is a bright sunny day, the kind of day I remember when I was much younger. Although it was a different time, the sunlight and day still look the same as I recall my past days upon the deck of a Navy ship. I'm pulled back into the future, as I see my ride pull into my driveway. I walk out quickly and sit in the car. I then comment. "This seat is not very comfortable". The reply from the driver seat is a usual, " You always say that" Nick, the driver, and car owner thinks to himself, "These seats feel great. What he misses is his wallet."

I look down at my electronic pad and say to myself "Where's my wallet? Something seldom seen. Today it has been replaced by the electronic pad. This device is used to communicate and also for payment transactions. The device also markets commercial advertisements based upon what I buy and what they think I should buy and of course I sarcastically think about my absolute favorite use; my place of employment uses this item to monitor my location.

At one time I would seek out what I needed. Now there is no need to since the companies that market products know what I need and regularly remind me of that fact.

At one time paying bills involved writing a check and using a calculator to make sure my accounts balance. Now this is not necessary since my pay is directly deposited and bills are automatically paid from the same account. The account starts and returns to where its balance began every month without having to do a thing.

Calling in when you are late for work is a thing of the past also. They know when I will get there and will let me know if I'm going to be late. They also know where I stop in the morning. My pad will handle that. As I shift nervously around in the seat, Nick takes notice and speeds up a little. But then he slows back down to the original speed he was travelling at. We have to be careful. Years ago you had to be on the lookout for the local sheriff or cop. Now they know how fast you are traveling without leaving their chair. Nick says, "No need for another email with an infraction and fine." I nod my head and just sink back into the seat and say "Like good little sheep". Nick chuckles.

We pull into the train station and choose a space, which seems like miles from where we need to go, but who can complain, as we are not running too late and the day is quite nice. I still can't resist commenting, "We could have walked from my house and been closer."

As we exit the car I hear the familiar beep of Nicks PDA. Nick replies, " I still can't get used to this, but it is easier than remembering to take the paper envelope off the windshield and mailing in a check for parking."

As we walk to the platform Nick comments, "You know you really should have an active "My-book" account. My reply is as usual, "I like to see or hear those I communicate with. I am not comfortable posting and reading and seeing a shadow, or an echo of the life of those people I choose to communicate with. I want to know them and speak to them."

His reply was a usual, "Well, I understand all that, but it does not look good to the company. They review your social media regularly and if you don't keep it up to date and have appropriate content they are not happy."

I grunt and shrug and just think to my self. "Appropriate content, their content not mine." I also think to myself about how I really feel and then again think to myself, " Well, let's not go there now, at least, while I am still working there,....or anywhere for that matter."

The train pulls up and we stepped aboard. We find a couple of seats, that's quite a treat. As I sink into the plush cushions, both of our pads beep simultaneously, letting us know that we bought a train ticket. I let out a grunt and lean a little to the left in a slightly defiant gesture, as if the invisible wallet in my rear pocket was uncomfortable as my weight shifted upon it. Nick chuckles a little and shakes his head, no one else seams to notice.

Chapter 2

- - -

Travel

I always enjoyed traveling, whether on a train or driving in a car. These days though my travel has been limited to the train, bus and getting a ride. You see a while back I had a problem with traffic enforcement, or at least they had a problem with me.

Sitting next to me was a young man reading a car magazine with the latest models. I glanced over and made a comment. " I liked the old ones better." He looked up and said, " What was your favorite car? "

I could not resist the opportunity to tell a story, so I said to him, " I will tell you, but it's part of a bigger story."

He said, "Ok, it's a long ride on the train, I have time."

So, I began,

I said, "Being used to doing what I usually do, I stopped at a place that I had been s visiting regularly for a Friday night couple of drinks. That night on the way home I drove through a check point; and even though I knew I was alright to drive, as I had been for years and was clearly under the legal limit to drive, I was behind the times as far as what the current law is as it applies to ME.

The young man piped in; "I know what you mean. I have been in that position before, sweating if you will make the limit even though you know you will be OK."

, I said " Exactly," and continued the story, "Since I am over 65 years old, the old standard that I was used to no longer applied. People over 65 years old are not allowed to have any alcohol in their systems, none at all while driving even though those between the age of 25 years old and 64 can be tolerated at .005 %. Well I was considered driving while impaired and therefore I was subject to the standard $25,000 fine and/or confiscation of my vehicle and I ended up in court.

Well, when I was younger I was all too busy with my life and family. I did not pay attention to when the first law based upon age was imposed. I did not listen to a dear friend of mine whom I had known for years.

My friend Isaac often says that, "You have to be mindful of the present, because small things now will result in bigger issues later. Things just seem to expand tremendously over times especially when they are not good things and the government is involved."

I continued, " You see when I was younger we were all equal, this was prior to the conditioning of the media.

Then years later someone had a good idea how to control a problem with underage drinking and driving. The idea was to have a zero alcohol tolerance for these drivers. Everyone thought it was a good idea and it apparently worked based upon the statistics provided by the government."

The young man piped up," Yes, I know I was subject to that rule."

I Continued," We were not conscious of the fact that once you create a subclass of citizens you open the door to more subclasses of citizens. After a few years this sub-classification continued and expanded to those of genetic background who historically showed a low tolerance to alcohol. So the government decided that, mainly the indigenous people of the Americas who lived here prior to European settlers arriving were subject to the law. They cannot have alcohol in their possession, or in their home because that is a crime. They would need an alcohol tolerance of lower than zero in order to drive.

Children learn mostly by example, not direction. So all these kids who grew up under this new law took sub-classification of the citizens and different rules as the norm. They did not learn, nor had they experienced that we are all equal and although they heard this in school they did not live it. When they took charge of the country and came of age they visualized and resolved problems in the only way they were familiar with.

Another new subclass now involved me, that is: folks over 65 years of age. Because their reactions are now considered slower than the average population, they were considered inferior drivers. Even though most of these folks did much for the community, they were no longer to be tolerated for the "greater good". My friend Isaac grew up in Nazi Germany and barely escaped with his life. He could tell you quite a bit about the "greater good", but let's not go there for now. The young man looked puzzled for a minute then continued to concentrate on the story. What puzzled him was how someone I knew could have lived in Nazi Germany since all that took place 100 years ago.

Oh, yes about that fine? Fortunately, the judge was lenient and did not impose the $25,000 fine. He knew I was trapped in a new age that I was not comfortable with. There was nothing either of us could do about this issue unless it resolved itself by my generation dying off. Unfortunately, he had no choice but to suspend my license and to confiscate my 1990's era antique vehicle, a Mercedes, and a name brand not often heard of anymore and even harder to find parts for. Since it still used gasoline as fuel and was leaving my ownership and you cannot own a car without a license, I would have to transfer it to my wife. However, as it was no longer grandfathered for public highway use and was no longer considered to be roadworthy. It had to be destroyed solely because of the fuel it used.

A car is a car and I will not miss it for that reason. I will miss gazing into the back seat through the rear view mirror and seeing the fleeting images of my girls when they were toddlers. I did get my license back, but as a protest I never bought a car again. My wife still had her car that was not quite as old as the Mercedes. It was just the annoying whine of an electric motor that got to me, but it was the means of a ride when I needed one."

The young man commented, " I never thought about it twice. I just figured when I grew up I would not be subject to the rule anymore. I never thought that later in life I would be back in the same position. I did not think twice when they enacted the laws against the elderly. You are right. It really isn't fair to judge all people by the lowest common denominator. Government and society just started taking things away from you."

I said, " Yes, you're right and it is not the idea of having a drink and being able to drive that really bothers me, although that is the symptom, it is the dignity of being equal and treated like everyone else. Once you are no longer equal it is very easy for that inequality to be expanded. "

The young man nodded and as he did the train bumped and pulled into Grand Central Station. We exited the train, made our way on to the platform and onto the street.

Chapter 3

- - -

Family

As I walk down the street I hear a familiar beep. It is a text from one of my daughters. I immediately responded with a hello and as usual we did all the dad stuff, how are you etc. We communicate, but we cannot really say what is on our minds, at least not over text, or the phone. You see these services are monitored. I would never want to get into a discussion of political views and what I think of the world on her text account, or phone. She has a long bright future ahead of her and I would do nothing to mess that up by having controversial information appear on her account. We do however have a code. Like any type of imposed controls either by the government, or society, people will find a way around a problem and I am sure my family is not alone.

If she says, "I think the sun will break through the clouds," she needs me. I will do what it takes to actually see her in person where I can help her out with the situation at hand. If she says, " I think I may see a movie this weekend with a friend, did you hear anything about this movie?" This means all is well. She is going to the movies this week so there are no worries for now.

At one time you could discuss issues under protected status. One old-fashioned term a wife cannot be made to testify against her husband was an example.

These freedoms are long gone as is the ability to discuss things with clergy, or your counsel in confidence. Our individual protections all fell mute at the beginning of the century as part of the mandatory reporting of certain types of behavior or incidents to the government. This was then expanded to any incident, or spoken word that might be considered illegal, or potentially dangerous and was finally further expanded by the monitoring and recording of all electronic communications by the government.

These communications are monitored by the government as are private companies contracted to listen, view and categorize information. The main clients of the contracted companies are insurance companies and other private industry. They use this information to monitor the behavior of the insured clients and industry employees. They regularly produce reports that are distributed to the appropriate paying party.

Again, there is a place for everything and I am sure a good reason behind all laws, but it is still a great concern that all individuals, the little people, are now truly isolated and left to their own devices to sort out their issues regardless of who, or what they are. This is all a result of our past stewardship. Again those kids grew up and just took action and made decisions in government based upon what they were exposed to by society.

Thinking of her also I texted my other daughter. I pulled another phone out of my pocket, after a quick look around, I walked over to a large grate containing a huge transformer, this should do it.

There is no need for code where she lives. I text "How are things going." She sometimes takes a while to get back to me. She works for the Navy as a WAVES. This time there was no delay. She texts back, " I am fine. I'm relaxing at home." She then continued," You and Isaac really gave me a hard time today. Cooperation and listening, lol."

I said, "Yep it does come back around, lol. I remember a little girl who also had her own mind too."

She texts back, "Yep, I know the apple and the tree."

I then text, " I have to run into work text you later."

Chapter 4

- - -

Our weekly meeting

On Tuesday our company always has a weekly meeting. One of the things they expect you to do is text in your thoughts to Sara, the manager who usually conducts our meeting and is responsible for us. I often do not text in. I believe in living in the moment and it is better to be more spontaneous. Besides, why give someone ammunition to think about. I do however contribute, only in real time.

Sara begins with social media and " How is everyone today?", she begins, but does not leave any space for anyone to answer the questions. She just continues, "As an employee, your responsibility is to promote business personally and as part of your duties." I think to myself, "Ok, now what," and lean a little forward in my seat waiting for the rub.

Sara is in her mid-twenties and the ideal pick for this position by the company. She is still traveling with enough momentum from her collegiate experience regarding what is politically correct so that she doesn't question what is expected of her. She is a true product of the age and thinks nothing of dealing with issues regardless of how they conflict with my reasoning and ethics of the past. She has a pleasant attitude and is not disliked by me even though a lot of what she professes is quite alarming and foreign to me.

Sara continues " As you know, the company officially promotes My-Book as the our official social media provider. You can have other social media providers, but you must have a My-Book account and we expect postings about us. "

I think to myself, "Yep, that is what I was waiting for."

She continues " As you also know it is a condition of employment that you agreed to as part of your employment contract and we have the right to enforce this." Now, I roll my eyes a little and think. A contract? I always thought a contract was composed of negotiation between two parties in which they come to an agreement of what is tolerable and "fair". This employment contract is more or less placed in front of you, or emailed to you and you are expected to read it and agree. It is not up for negotiation. You sign the contract papers or agree electronically on the web that you have read it and that was it. I lean a little more to the side and she continues. Again this was another conditioning she received in school. Those regulations or "contract with the school regarding behavior" is the guiding force here. She thought that if you want to go to school, or to the prom, or whatever public function you wish to participate in, then here is the contract, no negotiation, sign it or face the consequences of not participating. The forces of power impose their will upon you with no negotiation and you accept our rules.

Sara explains, "Checking your account and posting updates twice a day will be adequate. Keep your postings light and mention us and what we do where ever you can."

At this point I'm feeling a little annoyed and lean a little to the left in my seat. That imaginary wallet is causing me discomfort again, my little personal act of defiance.

Sara continues with a message from Human Resources. "Our company's monitoring contractor also contacted human resources and advised them of a few things they have seen. This relates to some of our younger associates, and some seniors." I quickly gaze off to the side to deliberately avoid her eye contact, in the event she was referring to me in the latter.

Sara goes on, "We just want to remind you that you are responsible for the personal content of your social media. If you post pictures or any content that we feel is objectionable, you can be subject to disciplinary action. I will gloss over the obvious violations, but want to bring a up few items, some new and some that have been a concern in the past. These new objectionable postings do include scenes from the beach that include the human form wearing less than what you are expected to wear for business attire." I raise an eyebrow and think to myself how postings will become a lot more boring.

She continues " Scenes that include religious content are also now considered objectionable. As you know we do not advise which religions you can belong to, but we also do not want any religious content at all associated with our company as some clients may view this to be offensive. "

I say to myself, "Wow, I'm glad my kids are older, because there goes Christmas Day pictures and the old Christmas tree. My friend's grandsons Bar Mitzvah that I am invited to in a few months is also out now too."

The next topic was appropriate clothing at work. Sara continued, " Although I am not going to require any women associates to cover their head, we have changed our policy regarding pants. In the interest of keeping up with current acceptable trends in business, the Company now requires that all ladies refrain from wearing pants and shorts at work, unless it is a sports function or beach setting where pictures will not be taken. Dresses and skirts of adequate length are now our acceptable norm here and we will be instituting that policy officially the first of next month. This will allow everyone time to adjust her wardrobe accordingly.

I just sat back and said "Wow" to myself, "It just keeps getting better."

Sara continues with a few dozen more issues. My mind floats off a little, but I still pay enough attention in the event that something really important, or blatantly intrusive is mentioned.

She then closes the meeting with "We don't want to be too intrusive in your lives, but do want it to be clear of what we expect of all of our staff."

I stood up looked around and then walked down the hall to my manager's office for my weekly meeting. Sara caught up with me, she stopped me and says, " Doug has to see you, and he has something important to discuss with you. It has to do with your public records and the Internet."

I said, "Ok, I'm on my way to see him now".

Sara also continues," After your meeting text me, we need to have a meeting also. Text me and let me know when you are free and I will set it up."

I said, " Ok I will." While I was really thinking to myself here we go. This will be one of those situations I am sure will end badly.

Chapter 5

- - -

Chance meeting

While walking through the break room I ran into one of the factory inspectors, Mike. Mike always seemed to be in his own world. Today he was a little more off-center than usual.

I then said, "Well, Mike, what is the matter? Did Africa get to you the last trip?" He had just returned from Kenya.

Seeming disinterested, but still annoyed as usual at my comments he replied.

"No not Africa, the management of this place."

I looked at him and chuckled then said, "Well you're finally starting to catch on aren't you? I figured that out quite a few years ago".

He then responded as if I had said nothing with more of a rant of frustration than an explanation.

Mile exclaimed. " That Kenya plant is overproducing and that's impossible. I know they cannot produce what I see and every time I am there the numbers don't fit. I even saw a truck with Somali markings pull out of the plant as I arrived. This is what I get paid to do, to verify that all production is within the plant and not from elsewhere for quality standards control."

He then continues, "Then I find out that they could be receiving production from a Somali plant to bolster our Kenya plant's production. You and I know along with everyone else in the world that this is not allowed. Somalia is a banned nation for imports to the U.S and most other nations. There on the loading dock is a huge truckload of stuff, coming into our plant with our markings and labeling. So I'm not supposed to notice this!"

I looked at him, made a face of disgust and let him continue.

Mike then says, " I come into work early to explain to my superiors what I found and rather than being interested that I did my job properly and agreeing that they will look into it, I get this reaction that appears to make me a trouble maker."

Then I get a look of unbelief and the comment, "Are you sure."

Punctuated by "Let's not jump to conclusions, etc."

I looked at Mike and said, "I wish I could help, but I have to go see Doug."

I'll be in mid-town close to here. Let's have lunch and talk about it and decide who is the biggest idiot in this place."

Mike looked at me and smiled. During these lunches he never spoke much, but was always amused as I went off on tangents about how stupid people are and how they ever got their jobs. We always finished lunches with our spirits a little lifted by venting on the issues that we can't do anything about out in the open. Also Mike knew that I would never snitch, nor he on me to H.R about our derogatory comments about other employees.

He said, "The usual place."

I said "Yep, the one near Isaac ".
He then smiled and said, "Crazy Isaac!"

Chapter 6

\- - -

Doug, my manager

Doug is a product of the new age and is responsible for motivating all in his charge, not that he has to motivate me. He actually spends very little time on the topic of productivity and sales, that's what I actually do and I am quite good at my job. His main task is to keep me within reach and on the right path regarding policy. That is quite an arduous task for him.

Doug has been managing me for about three years, taking over from my old manager Kelly as part of the acquisition of the company. For the first six months it did not go very well, at least for him. We had our issues regarding policy. I thought for a while though I was a goner, but was actually saved by my customers.

My customer base has been with me for some time. I do my best to get the best deal for the company as my customers vie for their best deal also. It is a sport between us to compete in a gentlemen's way "to one-up the other", without causing harm to our business relationship.

Well, the company had some ideas of replacing me. While on my mandatory vacation, they marketed my accounts as a precursor to the inevitable. Well it did not go as the company planned. My customer base for the most part rebelled and made it clear that they do business through me and that any change will not be accepted.

The company had no choice and I was secure for the moment although placed on probation and in the charge of Doug. The company was also clear that we both succeed, or we both fail together.

Well this made Doug face reality. This was what I had been waiting for all along. It all culminated in a meeting with Doug expressing his dismay in hushed hostile tones. Yelling at subordinates of the company was no longer acceptable. He asked me if I was trying to get him fired, my response of course was "no", then with a little of my humor, "Well I don't think so."

He softened a little and explained how he needs this job and he has a family with a wife who is expecting. I being a romantic said, "Ok, I will TRY to do what is expected of me socially."

I continued to say, "You should know how hard that is for me, or anyone of my generation."

(That was the generation that saw the late Neil Armstrong walk on the moon and fought WWII. We'll get back to that later.)

I said "Since you now ask me like a gentleman and you need me, I will do my best to comply."

After that he knew how to reach me and I knew that he was being REAL with me, at least most of the time. Our relationship was much better from that point on except for a few bumps in the road of course. I did my best even though I still own and wear shoes that I bought new, that were older than his grandfather would be today if he were still alive. (Again we will get back to this later.)

Although today Doug looked a little worried so I asked him, "Well, what did I do or not do now."

Doug said, " HR contacted him with an honor violation on your paperwork and the web records."

I said, "An honor violation?" I stood there with the look of a question mark on my face.

He continued, "The paperwork that you filled out indicates that you were born in 1962."

I said "And what is wrong with that?"

Doug continued, " One of the contractors that's work for HR does random probes into information validity, and they indicated that you were born in 1925." This was based upon facial recognition software that randomly probes the public space of the Internet and social media.

I sat back for a minute and felt shocked that this great Internet and social media network bagged me once again. I usually was pretty careful about what got on line about me. There were only a few pictures that really got into the public space. The one in particular I was thinking about was on the Battleship Missouri a while back when the Japanese surrendered.

Then feeling a little flush coming on I said, " 1925! WHAT ARE THEY NUTS, I would be over 120 years old?"

With that comment I looked into the glass window of his office to get a possible reflection of myself.

I continued, "I know I did not age well as opposed to other people my age, but saying I look like I'm over 120 years old IS DOWN RIGHT INSULTING."

Doug smiled a little and said, " I don't think you look THAT old. They want to see you and so does Sara. If I were you I would talk to them directly and straighten this out. It has to be a mistake."

I looked at him and said, "I know she got me in the hallways after the meeting. You know how I am looking forward to this, NOT. She is all right as a person, but I always feel I am sinking deeper into quicksand when I talk to her."

Doug continued, " They also have indicated that you have attended two high schools and two colleges. Both at different times and dates, totally impossible."

Now he was staring at me and he could sense that this was bothering me.

I sat there and began feeling a little out in the open, but I thought about it and came up with a line to take the attention off the moment. " Well did I get good grades, or am I in trouble for that also?"

Doug smiled and moved on with other items to discuss.

Doug had a few more items as usual and when I thought I was finally free he introduced me to Steven. Steven was a young kid maybe 26 years old and new to the company.

I was polite and said hello and not missing the opportunity said, " Who is this, my new manager?"

Doug smiled and could not help to giggle a little and said, " No, we haven't succumbed to that around here yet. He is a new salesman and we want him to go out with you because you possess strong personal skills with the clients."

I said with a smile, "Well kid, pay close attention and you will be sitting in HR with me before you know it."

Of course, this went right over Steven's head and he just stood there with a bewildered look on his face. I looked up at Doug and he at me and we both looked at the ceiling and shook our heads a little.

Doug asked Steven to step out side for a minute and then he said, " So are we ok with this?"

I looked up and said, "Sure, I'll take him around and teach him."

I know you have to give to receive and Doug needed me so I will help for the next time I need him, which could be a lot sooner than one might expect.

At the end of our meeting Doug said in a hushed course tone as I was getting up. "Now remember behave yourself, don't be a knucklehead today with HR, you will straighten it out."

Doug knows I love that 1930 vernacular expressed by gangsters in movie shows and of course that Holy Grail, my favorite comedians of the day, the stooges.

I gave him a smile and slipped out the door.

Chapter 7
- - -
Lunch.

Well, Mike stood us up, or a least I thought he did. I sat and waited, then tried to call him. His pda has no voice mail, as his number did not work. His office extension had no message as if it was an un-initialized extension.

We sat for a while and spoke.

Steven then said, " What was it like when you first started to work at the company?"

Seeing an opportunity for a story I could not resist.

I pushed back in the chair and began, " When I first started working here it was different. We the "sales people" were more in control of our schedule and methods. As long as you sold, you were accepted providing there was nothing illegal going on and the customers were happy."

> I then said, " Prior to working here things were much different. There was no My-book book, or any social media for that matter. If you went back just a little further from that no email. You had a mobile phone and that was it, if you could afford one since they were much more expensive."

Steven sat and I could tell he was wondering just by the expression on his face.

Seeing I had his attention I continued, "I felt we were the masters of things. Government was not deeply involved in our lives as long as you paid your taxes. You could find a good or crummy job all the same depending what you wanted. Then the world just changed one day."

I continued, " We were all lulled into a semi sleep by what we surrounded ourselves with, cars, television, appliances, vacations, that's all we concerned ourselves with. We did not see the subtle changes that took us down the path we are on now.

Steven then said, "It's not so bad; we are still a free nation."

I just looked at him and could feel a wave of discontent, anger, a mixture of both, but I took a breath and further explained myself. "True that is what they tell us, but let's look at the facts. Exactly how free are you if those who are watching you know everywhere you go, who you are associating with, and all the other intimate details of your life that come out of the data-mining information age. It is even harder for those who are dependent on the government and cannot get a break."

Steven then said, "Oh you mean the uneducated and unmotivated."

I looked over at him and said, " Yes and no. Yes because they are those of us of whom we are speaking and no, the description you are providing is not truly accurate. There was a time when experience was far more important than a degree. People would work for just about nothing just to gain experience. Today it is different. Even if you worked in a job for many years you still are not qualified for it if you wanted to apply for the same job in another company. It is just wrong. Thomas Edison created that big conglomerate based around his ideas and inventions. He had no college degree. Edison was home schooled educated by his mother. If he applied to work at this company today, even with all of his experience, accomplishments and ideas, without a degree he would not even get a second look. Isn't there something wrong with this?"

Steven sat back and thought about it, awed by the whole idea of being schooled at home.

I then said, " I have nothing against school if used properly. Obviously, you need some type of training for what you plan to do as a career. My issue is that this is the only answer and there is a reason. The liberal thinkers of the day want one last shot at you before you go out into the world, to turn your mind to their way of thinking. You are subjected to multiple years of influence in what they feel are correct ideas and behavior. When you finally leave it takes years for the effects to dissipate for some and for others it never does. That is why we are in the shape we are in. There are no value judgements being brought into the world. Only ideas that really don't work in real life, but we have to pretend they do. For all those people who did not partake in the process, life is much more difficult. You are an outsider and are lucky to have someone throw you a crumb. You can be the best worker in the whole division or area of the company, but you keep your mouth shut and fly low. Stand out and someone may find out you were not part of the system and you can be done before you started."

This is how it works for elected officials also. Your personal finances could be in a complete mess. You could not manage a dollar if you tried, but if you are part of the right team, you are OK. You could be pitted against a business person with experience and accomplishments and you will still win because you have the team and the votes. People who vote really don't think. If you are not very successful in life do you want to vote for someone like yourself? This is usually what happens. Or do you want to vote for someone who can really do the job and make changes happen that you need to make your life better. Now this same person who could not run his own finances is helping to run the whole country. No wonder why the municipal budgets just don't work.

People just love to vote gifts out of the treasury for themselves, but remember nothing is free. You may think that the government money, or subsidy is free, but it is not.

You now are beholden to keep voting for the team that will keep these things in place because you lost the ability to live on your own. They give you enough money to barely survive and you do nothing. Then your self-confidence goes and you are truly empty and you become a slave.

Give a man or women a decent job, not even a high paying one, enough money to rent an apartment or buy a small house, own a car or two with enough money left over to live. They can now raise a family, maybe a vacation once in a while and you just created a free thinker who will vote for what is truly best for the country. Only important issues would be undertaken. All the fluff and indentured voting would be gone along with those in government to promote this system of government.

Remember once the majority of people are on the government dole you can never change it back. History has taught us this.

Also, there are people in the world who only accept one truth. There is no room for a difference of opinion on a subject. This is the case and your opinion does not matter if it is not in lock step with the public platform. You either stay in step with the program or you will be cast out as freedom of speech and ideas only apply to theirs and if your ideas are not theirs then your ideas and you are inferior."

As I finished that last line I looked up at the TV and saw the breaking news that Mike, my co-worker, had been killed. I was in shock and disbelief as the monitor in the luncheonette flashed the images and a commentator talked about the story. My PDA also was flashing similar commentary, and then I received an odd message.

A text from Isaac, it said, "I have to go somewhere quickly, see me now if you want an order." I texted back, "OK".

As I left the Luncheonette, I did not see the breaking news that the person they were looking for was me. I was walking, or more so wandering in deep thought thinking how this could have happened? Who would do this and why?

I wandered down the street as my PDA continued to chime as the news unfolded. I was not paying attention although Steven was. He said to me, "It's on the news that you killed Mike." I did not hear him at first as I was thinking about what happened. Then I stopped and stood in disbelief of the fact that Mike was no more.

We then walked past a driveway near the back of Isaac's building. I then heard a voice. "Stop, this way I don't have time, hurry we have to go." I walked down the alley, Isaac reached out to what I thought was to shake hands, but instead grabbed my PDA, flipped it over, opened the battery door dislodging the battery and a very old looking silver plastic covered card that fell to the ground. It looked like one that would hold a baseball card, except it was mirror plastic with no markings. He looked at the card, looked at me and said, "Not such a good hiding spot is it." He picked the card up handed it to me and also handed me the parts of the pda, now three parts a battery, a battery door and the device itself.

Isaac then looked at me and he had an odd expression on his face. I had recently cut my hair short and grew a small beard since I saw him last.

I said, " Well are you going to punch me out or ask me out on a date?"

Isaac giggled and said, " Sorry, you reminded me of someone for a minute."

Isaac said, " Follow me". Then he said," You should pay more attention to the news".

As Steve chimed in, " Yes, I saw the news."

I looked at him and said, "Good morning, now you are awake."

I replied " I did see the news, someone killed Mike".

Isaac said, " Yes someone did and everyone thinks it is YOU".

Isaac then says, "Everyone except me that is".

Then Steven chimed in again, " Me also."

Isaac and I looked at each other again, just a gentle head shake left and right from the both of use and we continued into the back door of his building where we could figure out our next move.

Chapter 8

- - -

My Customer Isaac

Truly he is one of my favorites. No one knows how old he is, or me for that matter, as he is off the grid in regard to information. This is intentional on his part as it is with me.

One of his favorite lines is, " They can't get you if they don't know you exist." A good method to live by as it worked for him in the past. What I do know is he lived in Germany in the 1930's and barely made it out alive with most of his family.

He's vibrant especially for his age and as some other salesmen who fill in for me from time to time describe him as "CRAZY".

He always starts our meeting with, "Well, what did you do this week that upset Doug and did you get him fired yet?" I replied as usual, "Not yet, but the day isn't actually over yet either is it?"

With a smile we go about our business. He always has a tidbit about himself every week some more some less. We would often talk about his escape from Nazi Germany, or his service in the US Navy. This is where I first met Isaac. Even though time was short I took time to tell Steven the story, since we were all now irreversibly connected by the events of today.

Prior to departing on board our first ship the battleship, "USS Washington", (This is also where we both met my daughter for the first time), Isaac and I did not know each other yet nor did we know that she was my daughter. However she knew both of us and kept Isaac and my first meeting in the future aboard the ship, as it was intended to be. It was an interesting relationship since she was twice my age of 16. She also helped sneak me into the Navy because I was underage. I would turn of age in a few months, but rather than leave me hanging around on the streets of the City she helped me enlist at my request.

I always thought of her as an older aunt trying to straighten me out, although she knew from experience that this was impossible. It was not until years later when I saw her grow up that I knew who she actually was. I have a picture of us just before I shipped out. She stayed behind at the induction center, and honored my request to keep silent regarding who she actually was when she met us before her appearance in the future time period. Years ago I managed to send her back to 1942 where I knew she would be safe.

Steven just looked at both of us like he just blew a fuse in his head. He had no understanding of what we were talking about and did not want to even try.

Isaac then continued, "We were assigned to a battleship that was quite a prize, the USS Washington. Later in the war we were both transferred to the USS Missouri. Being a crewman on a battle ship was the ultimate for a young kid from Bridgeport, Connecticut, or Brooklyn, New York for that matter "

Isaac then said, " We were there on the Missouri when the Japanese surrendered.   Bring that picture up on your pda."

I then stated," Yep, that is the picture that landed me in hot water with Sara and the HR department."

Steven did and Isaac was quick to point out the two of us in the front row of the sailors witnessing the event. Steve them mumbled, "But how was that possible?"

I also said, " I did not realize what an honor it was until I received a letter from my aunt. I had sent her the standard picture the Navy takes of you in your uniform, along with a picture of the ship. If you are willing to pay for it they will also give you a picture of the ships you served on with your name and highest rank printed on it.   My Aunt proudly brought the first and later the second picture to the drug store. This drugstore was the place where people were able to get a good cheap meal especially if they were in a hurry.

On another wall of the dinning room were pictures of everyone serving, or killed in action.   Even though the wall was quite full, she thought they would eventually put it in one of the remaining spaces. " When she returned a couple of days later, my picture and ship where located in the center of the wall. " This was quite an honor back where I grew up."

Isaac continued, "We met when we were on deck and I was talking to Willie one of the Black mess hall hands when he heard a commotion. He got off his stool and walked over and saw a number of guys razzing me about being a Jew and Willie about being black. Even though he never met someone who was Jewish, or for that matter went out of his way to have a conversation with someone who was black, it infuriated him that Willie and I (Isaac) were being mistreated. He stood up adjusted his sailor's hat and walked right into trouble. "

Then I chimed in, "Something that I am still good at today."

Then Isaac continued and said that I said, " What's the matter with you guys? Why are you bothering them for, they can't help who they are?"

Then Isaac said, "When he said it I was little insulted at first, but then I understood he was a hardhead expressing how he felt and was trying to help."

The leader of the crowd said, " What's it to you?"

Isaac continued and said " He stood and looked at the leader, cocking his head in a manner that was quite derogatory and just did not answer.

I then piped in, " Something I do pretty regularly at work, but people just don't get the gesture any more and just look at me bewildered."

Isaac continued, "The leader then said, "Well I'm in the mood for a fight, so I will just start with you."

Isaac said "I took this as an invitation and then in short order finished the three of them off, It was simple, all three and with a few quick punches the three found themselves on the ground and hurting."

Isaac then said, "You looked quite pleased with how things turned out, nodded at Willie and me, then proceeded back to his seat."

Willie nodded back and headed into the kitchen. I followed him back to his chair sat down and Isaac said, "Well, you're a handy guy to have around aren't you."

He looked up at me and said, " Yes I can be."

Thinking back about the unpleasant events of the current day Isaac leaned back in his chair and smiled.

Steven then said, Was it much different living in Germany back then? Isaac then looked directly at him with a serious look. He then exclaimed, " You tell me, YOU TELL ME what it was like, you are living through the beginning of it now!"

He further explained " The control, the monitoring, the ability to see everything you do and say, thank god they can't hear what you think, they would have fired him, years ago." He was of course pointing at me. I broke a little smile over that one.

Isaac then said, "Thank god Hitler did not have half the stuff they have to keep an eye on you today. If he did none of us would have made it out alive and you would be speaking German or Japanese right now."

He then said to both of us, "What is the price of freedom?"

Steven was not able to answer so Isaac continued and did not look at me because I already knew the answer, "To protect us all from someone, to do something. Is saving one life, 10 lives or all of our lives, Is it worth the price of our freedom? Is the means to do so worth our freedom, when When WHEN? That is the question I have for you, WHEN? "

I looked up at him as I could not resist since Steven did not have the answer and said, "Life without freedom is life without hope. To truly have freedom is worth the risk of all our lives."

Isaac looked at me raised his hands palms up toward the ceiling and then exclaimed, " I am glad someone has been paying attention to what I have been saying all these years, YOU ARE CORRECT. There always has to be a loophole, or it has to be rough around the edges for things to work for you, me, or THE WORLD. When you close all the loopholes and polish everything up we all lose. Things just get too tight, no air." As he said it he looked at me with a smile, his gold front tooth glistening in the office light.

It is no longer the norm with visits to customers. Most associates now communicate primarily through email and some, believe it or not, order through text. It is so impersonal and anonymous. Some do more business than I, some do less. The company prefers this type of electronic transaction as they can see everything you both say and write. The one place where this type of sales falls short is, the absence of a business relationship. There are no stories to be told, or interaction other than just business, not that I waste time, only enough to keep things where they should be.

As a result sales turnover of customers is high and changing a salesman is easy. Who knows who is on the other end of the text or email, until they tell you.

Some customers complained that the new salesmen were still using the prior salesman's email for several months and they didn't know there was a change. My visit today to a customer and a friend proved that.

I know my time is numbered in my way of conducting business with my clients, but won't worry about that for now. I have bigger problems.

Isaac then said, " We must leave". Then he motioned for us to get into one of his vans. I quickly jumped in along with Steven.

As I sat in the back on a box, I asked, "Why are you helping me? This may get you in trouble. I'll tell them that I didn't do anything, just let me tell them that."

Isaac pushed back in the seat as he started the van into motion and let out a boisterous laugh saying, "They won't get me, they have been trying for years, even Hitler failed. You on the other hand are another story. They won't wait for a trial, you won't make it to trial."

He then looked at me in the mirror and said, " I must help you regardless to repay a debt, I debt I owe you and all of your kind. If it were not for you, I and part of my family would not be here today."

I sat back against the wall on the box against the wall and became silent.

Chapter 9

- - -

Steam tech of the day

Isaac then said," Well where are we going? Not home of course, they will be there."

He then reminisced about a battle we had and the computer got damaged on the Missouri and how I was able to fix it.

Steven said, "They had computers back then."

And I said, "Yes, but they were more of an adding machine with vacuum tubes, than a computer.

Isaac then said, "But none-the-less you fixed it when most of the tubes exploded from the shock of a blast. We were helpless without the aiming control computer because the ship moved with every salvo (firing of the three main guns). We would be off target every time we fired the guns. The computer calculated the movement of the ship and electronically adjusted the aiming system of the guns for the distanced traveled."

Seeing an opportunity for a story, I loved to tell stories, I continued. "Willie had broken a light bulb in the deck a few weeks earlier. He then tried to remove the bulb from the socket in the kitchen, there was no disconnect or light switch handy so he used a utensil and was shocked. The strange thing about it was the utensil was made of a hard plastic, or more so a ceramic which was able to conduct electricity. He came to get me since I was on a maintenance detail for my regular job on board and I changed the bulb

I marveled at the new lightweight kitchen utensils and asked if I could have a few of them to play around with how they conduct electricity. Willie filled a small sack with a few pieces and said, "Here you go."

Over the next few weeks I then found that some conducted electricity when others did not. Other types when pressed together, one side next to the others' would only allow direct current electricity to travel in one direction. I found this very interesting, but did not have the opportunity to tell anyone. I did however make a number of working models of this one-way electrical valve as I called it. One of the primary jobs of a power hungry fragile vacuum tube is to allow electricity to travel only in one direction, the same kind of vacuum tubes the ship used in its electronic firing controls.

Then Isaac said, "He took them with us when we were transferred to the Missouri. When some of the vacuum tubes we needed were broken and we had no vacuum tube replacements, this guy informed the captain and used about a dozen of these plastic ceramic pieces that he set up as an electric circuit. He fixed the aiming computer with them by replacing the broken vacuum tubes."

Isaac then continued, "Quite a feat, a feat of engineering and it earned you a few metals and a job at Gloom Lake a few years after the war."

Now it was like a light went off in Steven's head, He said, Gloom Lake that's Area 51, you actually worked there?"

Isaac and I both looked at him and smiled, Isaac looking in the back of the van while driving amid the sound of blaring horns from other upset drivers, as he ran into their lane or cut too close, the usual style of his driving.

Isaac then continued, "Yep he worked at Gloom Lake and then some."

Steve then said, " Are there real aliens in that place."

Seeing the opportunity to be a wise guy I said, "Well that depends. If you mean from other countries of the world yes, If you mean aliens from outer space no. "

Isaac, butted in, "Germans, that's who they have. The Nazi rocket scientists and techs. That's who worked there then, those murderers. They went there after the war to help fight the communists during the Cold War years."

I looked at him with an expression of annoyance at being interrupted again and continued, "The only aliens I ever met from outer space worked in the HR department of our company."

Isaac let out a chuckle and even Steve found some humor in this.

"There may be some hope for the boy after all." Isaac commented about Steven.

I then said, "We need to find a large transformer or power line. "

Steven then said with a perplexed look, "Why?"

I said, "Because I want to text my Daughter. "

Isaac, smiling, pulls over next to a large fenced in enclosure of transformers, knowing the drill.

I pulled the other phone out of my pocket and said "This should do nicely, there is a strong magnetic field here."

Steven then commented, " Magnetic field?"

I said, "Yes, the device only works when it is near a strong magnetic field - a power plant, large transmission line or transformers."

I also continued, "These magnetic fields act as an assist enhancing the device to compress the earth's natural magnetic field, which allows us to cause resonance on the "Higgs field". This resonance is what the devices receive and decipher for communications."

Steven looked at me and of all the things we had been talking about he got this. School focuses more on science and math than general common knowledge and that is why he would understand this kind of talk and would not have a clue with other simpler interpersonal issues.

I activated the transmitter and was instantly connected to her, although usually she could not answer that quickly

I texts, " I'm in a jam and need your help."

Fortunately she was available at my request because her home was by a transformer site and she text back, "What is wrong?"

I said, "Isaac and I are in a tight spot, I need you to contact me and ask me what to do. I cannot do it myself in this time. I never worked that problem out of the system. You can ask me in the future and see if I am still there."

She then said, " How, I usually answer your texts."

I said, "I know, but what I need you to do is look through my texts and reply to one that is in my future. If you don't have one handy, hit "properties" of the text and find the resonation number."

She texts," Ok I will. I have it."

I texts, " Show me the number."

She texts back,"1223.3334.9999.4040.9990.4830.9968.1415.1112."

I said, make a new text box and put that number in, with the change of the last 4 digits to 1319. This should put you in touch with me if I'm still around. Don't worry, I'll get right back if I am there I am waiting for your texts."

She texts back, " There is no response,"

I said " Isaac, we have to change our destination, we did not make it. Just picture doing something else and change the direction of the van."

Isaac did and 2 seconds later she text, " I have your text from you in your future."

I texts, "Well what did I say, how did I get out of it?"

She texts back, " Just do what Isaac wants to do. His new plan will work and you should be all right."

I texts back, " Ok," knowing that both Isaac and I were still figuring that out, but with a little help from the future it should work out.

Steven then said, " How did you just talk to your daughter in the 1940s."

I smiled a little and I could see I had Isaac's attention. He had been aware of my ability to do this for some time although it perplexed him.

I said, " The universe if full of dark matter, some know it as the "Higgs Field". What I was able to do was use this field, or matter as an antenna, and much like a radio wave transmits its signal across the countryside, I transmit my resonance, for so many words onto this field. It resonates and is projected through all time and space at the same time. Although I have never been off this planet I believe it goes to the far reaches of the galaxy all at the same time, in an instant. "

I also continued, " The way I control the noise created by this is to use different resonation numbers; otherwise every text we ever sent each other would happen at the same resonation or time and would become an unusable jumble of data. The phone tracks time in the form of the resonation number and that is how we contact each other and the conversation is relevant. Otherwise every text I ever sent her, or she sent me would happen all at the same time. The number indexes up automatically so that our text conversations are relevant to the time and space they are being made. We can control them manually. I have to be careful how much I use this thing, that is why I text instead of using the voice mode. If I overuse the resonance, it would be so strong it would stop working. I save voice for special occasions, birthdays etc, since its impact is much greater than text. The nice thing about this thing is you will never miss someones birthday again."

Steven just looked at me with his mouth open and Isaac did appear to still be in the dark over how it works.

 so Isaac just said. " But let's not forget about the baby's Navel."

I said, "Oh boy, you had to bring that one up, didn't you."

Isaac said, " Of course, it's my job."

I then continued, " Issac, you can tell this one."

When a Navy ship passes the equator there are many traditions that sailors keep on a ship. One in particular I was subject to was the Baby's Navel and you get a special card for this experience ."

He continued, " You line everyone up and blindfold them if they don't have their card with them, or never received one. This is after you choose a fat sailor with a big sloppy belly that you rub mayonnaise on. The guys have to put their blindfolded face and kiss the navel of the baby (the belly of a fat sailor). In this case it was Chief Igor Brunsen." He let out a giggle with this one.

Steven said, "What is so funny?"

Isaac continued, " Well when they are all done and before you take your blindfold off, the fat sweaty sailor turns around and drops his pants and it appears as if the guys just kissed his backside. Just seeing the look on some of these guys faces was worth enlisting."

I then said," Tell him what else happened when you set me up for this one."

Isaac said, " He, (pointing at me) then chased us guys who set him up around the ship for 15 minutes until general quarters sounded, we had some enemy planes coming in. That was one time I was glad to see the enemy."

Chapter 10

- - -

The Race to the moon

One of the benefits of being so old is the number of things you were able to do in your lifetime. A favorite was the Apollo program 1st stage propulsion system. Isaac liked this story, so he took the opportunity to tell it rather than by butting in as usual.

Isaac said, " The Saturn V rocket had a flaw on the first stage. The flaw was that the five engines would harmonize, synchronize, shake shimmy rattle and roll. This made the whole ship vibrate terribly and I'm sure with the rough trip it was into space something the astronauts would like to avoid.

It was very time sensitive. We were in a race with the Soviet Union to get to the moon and they started off ahead of us with sputnik in 1957, a beeping satellite. Even though all it did was beep, you could hear it in America when it traveled over us. This does not seem important now, but in 1957 in the United States of America it was like we were being invaded.

Not being able to afford the time to redesign the rocket engines that were being produced over 6 years they had a big problem. Now tell them how you fixed it," Isaac said.

I said, "I was washing salad in a calendar in my kitchen and there was the answer in front of me." Normally water flows in a circle around the sink's to the drain. Because of the design of the colandar, the holes and slits in it, the water flow is interrupted and the water randomly flowed into the drain without circling. I then knew I had an answer."

I took this idea and the colandar to the team leader. I showed him how it worked to stop sympathetic harmonization in the sinks water flow in the cafeteria and right away he got it and we moved on the idea from there."

I continued, "We made something much bigger with an engineered design and aligned placement of the holes and slits that would fit into the throat of the rocket motor and it worked. The test firing of a motor worked fine and subsequently the devices went into the next test rocket where the sympathetic vibration problem was gone."

Isaac then continued dodging traffic and vehicle horns, " And then tell him who you met."

I then said, " I was invited to all the publicity events with the astronauts and met them all."

Steven asked, " And Neil Armstrong?"

I said, "Yes and Neil also. When I met him I asked Neil to do me a favor if he could. I had a set of dog tags from a friend who always wanted to 'send us to the moon', as he supervised us. Could he bring them on his voyage? Neil, being a military man took the dog tags from my hand and said, I can't promise anything, but I will try."

I continued, " I watched the rocket lift off from the viewing stand in Florida. I did not know that in Neil's personal affects pouch he had the dog tags, next to the picture of his wife and kids. "

I was in the control room in Houston when he landed and set foot on the moon. My job was long over by this time. My part of the program being in the launch vehicle propulsion, but I was invited to attend none the less. When he stood the American Flag up on the moon with Buzz Aldren the dog tags were attached to the base of the post.

Through the grainy pictures I thought I saw something shiny at the base of the flag, but was not sure. Not until Neil looked at the camera and pointed at them after the flag was installed, then I knew.

I then muttered to myself, " Well look who sent who to the moon."

Out of the millions of people watching the broadcast Neil had a special message for me that he was able to complete the task I asked of him. That was the kind of guy he was. Even in the turmoil of the thousands of things he had to do he still took time for the little things that meant so much to a few people.

Chapter 11

- - -

How we stopped aging

I know everyone must be wondering by now why we were not affected by age and this included Steve. Steve stated the obvious, "How is it you both are so old?"

Isaac and I gazed at him and I said, " Let me tell the story, so Isaac can pay attention to his driving"."

I continued, " We stayed on in the Navy after the war, Isaac and I both participated in Operation Sandstone, the nuclear testing that took place in the South Pacific."

Isaac butted in," Yeah they set off these awful huge nuclear bombs and as a result guys got sick, radiation sickness you know."

I continued a little more annoyed again, " US Navy troops were used in the tests of which both Isaac and I participated. Often troops would have radiation sickness as a result of the testing. They tried a number of preventative measures on different troops, of which we participated in. The measures did not work, at least for the radiation, Guys still got ill. We did not notice that we stopped aging until years later, for me probably about the time of Sputnik. I was very bothered by this and took steps, to look older."

Steven said, "How did you do that?" I said, "Mostly women's platinum blond hair dye, I would brush small quantities into strategic placed in my hair. This made me look like I was graying."

Isaac chimed in, " I never did anything at all, let them think I was young, people would never find me, they would be looking for an older guy."

I continued to work for government contractors until the late 70's. At that time I felt I had to remake myself, so I moved to a town where no one knew me. I obtained a new birth certificate with a new birth date, reused my parent's names and was enrolled in High School and subsequently college. It was amazing how easy it was to do this. No one checked anything, although now it is turning out to be problematic. I was stupid. I should have changed my name, but I did not want to lose my heritage and never had any idea that someday we would be so connected socially that this would be a problem.

After college I also went to work for the government again. That is where I worked on programs as a new engineer. The programs I worked on were more electronic and marine based. This way I could avoid anyone who may know me from aerospace.

Steve then said, "That is where the communicator came from, right?"

I said, "Yes, you guessed it. It was a program they started then cancelled. Because it was not a big capital expense program I continued to play with it and completed it myself not telling anyone about it, I knew it would come in handy some day.'

I continued. " They were more interested in the time travel component of the program. You know you can reach and affect the Higgs field as we do, you could also use it as a baseline to move in time. They continued to experiment with it, although never with what they thought was success. Time travel is a very odd thing. The fact you try to do it affects time itself and outcomes. My success was limited although I obviously had a few minor successes and one major one.

Isaac then said, "You left a part out didn't you?"

I said, "Yes I did. Before I retired I worked on a defense program called blaze, super secret, I was in propulsion again, but involving the ocean and orbital. The orbital never made it into being because of possible malfunctions that could rain dangerous materials on the public by accident, but the ocean based system did go into production. That is where I worked."

I then continued, " That is when I was given my distress card and was informed to use it in the event of an emergency, since the technology I helped to develop was top secret and very dangerous."

Isaac said, " Yes a card to get you out of trouble, or end your troubles depending upon the situation."

He then said, "Don't you think it's time to use the card." He was referring to the card that I had neatly tucked in the battery compartment of my PDA. I felt it with my hand in my pocket as we drove as to check to see it was there, or at least by touching it, I may get an idea of what to do.

I then said, "Out in the open, far and away."

With that Isaac stopped the van in a not so nice part of town. I then commented, " Are you sure we want to stop here?"

Isaac said, "Yes, we need to sit for a while and think about this. You asked me to change my plan and that is when everything started working out for you again. This is the idea I had that made your radio start working again after I thought of it, when you daughter could reach you again because you were still around."

I then said in a wise guy manner, " Well I can't argue with that kind of logic."

Isaac led us into the lower basement stairwell of a building. We went through an outer door and to an inner locked door. With that he pulled a card out of his wallet (he still had a wallet and yes I was jealous). He held it next to the door lock and the door snapped open. As we walked through the door I commented, " It's a social club. Where did you ever find..., never mind I don't want to know.

The interesting thing about this place is that normally it is natural to look and see who is walking through the door. In this establishment, a term I use loosely, no one looked up, or even responded. It was as if no one noticed, but obviously they did.

Isaac then commented, " Don't be rude and do not look at people directly. This is the kind of place where people want their privacy. Noticing others is not acceptable."

Isaac then continued, "These people come here speak their mind in peace. No pdas are used in this room. You can come here to meet with people without the worries of someone looking over your shoulder."

I then commented, " Respects privacy. This sounds like my kind of place."

As I said that I looked at the walls and ceiling of the room; it had old copper screening attached to it in a decorative utilitarian fashion.

I then commented, " I remember this from the Navy days. See that screen. No signals are coming or going from this place. The screening blocks them."

We sat down and the waiter came out with a drink for Isaac automatically. Isaac looked at me and said, " He will have a manhattan on the rocks with plenty of cherries.

I could not resist and then said, " When you make my drink hold it next to the vermouth bottle and let the light shine through it into my glass as the mixer."

The waiter smiled a little and said, " Light on the vermouth" as he then looked at Steve, who replied, "We're not supposed to drink while on duty."

 Isaac and I gave him a look as if to say, that's the only problem I have to worry about today.

Then Steven reconsidered and said, "I'll have a beer."

We sat for a while and with a drink in my hand I continued to tell more stories, one of my favorite pastimes when with friends and family.

I then stood up and walked to the bathroom.

Chapter 12

- - -

A quick trip

As I stood in the dark decrepit space a man stepped out of the shadows. He said, "We need your help. It will just be a moment and we will be right back."

I looked at him and did not recognize the person, but had a good idea who he worked for. I then said, " What about my friends in the other room."

He said, " No one will notice, we will be right back."

Understanding this was a matter of no choice I said, " Ok, but I still need to use the bathroom."

He said, " If I were you I would wait. Where we are going is much nicer than this."

Hearing sound logic like that I abandoned my rule of never going on a trip without a stop to the bathroom first and we departed.

As if it were only a moment I returned. I walked back into the room and things had changed. The crowd of people was gone. I said, "Well, where did everyone go?"

Isaac looked at me strangely and said, " There was never anyone here but us to begin with. Would you like another drink?" As he did he held up an old bottle he had in his van and pointed to a paper cup that had been assigned to me earlier."

I looked at him and said, " No I'm good."

Then he commented, "You have a bandage on your head and you look 30 years younger."

I then being guarded said, " I cut my self in the bathroom and found a bandage. While I was in there I also washed up nicely."

Isaac did not believe me for one minute, but did not press the issue knowing that I must have had my reasons. Isaac and I had started aging again. We did not look like we are 120 years old, but like we were in our mid-sixties. I however now looked significantly younger and it troubled him, although he did not ask why.

With that Steven asked a few questions about my past.

Chapter 13

- - -

More about me

I was born and grew up in Bridgeport Connecticut. Quite a place to live in the 1920's. More or less a factory workers dream that turned in to a nightmare in the 1930's depression.

I lived with my mother and my aunt. My father, who was an electrician, was killed by an accident. It was a hard life for us, but for me not knowing any better, it was my life.

I often got into scraps with kids.

Steven then commented, " Is that where you learned to fight?'

I said, " Well yes and no. I had a little help from a friend and neighbor, first a neighbor who became a friend. You never heard about him. His name was Jack Johnson, a price fighter who spent some time living in Bridgeport, as part of getting away from it all.

He was older then and would watch me get taunted by the other kids from time to time. My aunt and mother would say turn the other cheek.

He saw me walking home one day with a black eye and said, "Why don't you fight back?"

I said, " I don't know how and my mother would not like it and I still have another eye!"

Jack then said, " I can't help with the mother not liking it, but maybe I can with the other."

Jack Johnson was tall even by today's standards at 6 feet in height. He was also very strong, a powerful black man who filled the room with his personality even without saying a word.

Steven then commented, " That is why you helped Willie isn't it?"

I looked at him and commented, "It is not the only reason, that another black friend had helped me once. It was not right for those guys to take advantage of Willie or Isaac regardless, but it was a factor."

I also continued, " Jack said I was a lightweight, so he would feed me a snacks after school and have me do work for him. I would split wood, cut rocks out of his lawn with a pick and other similar labor-intensive work. After about six months he thought I was coming along nicely and said

I repeated Jack's quote, "Since you have done so much to help me NOW I will show you a few things that would help YOU."

I continued, " In his basement which was a gym, he showed me that being flexible and limber was important along with just being outright strong. He did this through a serious of jumping and rolling exercises. He also showed me how to weave and when to lock up with an opponent, (grab heads and shoulders), and when to break away and just punch it out.

I continued, " I didn't notice it, but he did, I was growing and he was pleased.

After one of our sessions Jack said, " So I'm not telling you to fight, but when you need to you are ready. I looked and him and just smiled."

I continued, "About a week later I was walking home in a good mood. "

Jack was in his front yard. In his usual short manner he said, " I can see your face now LET me see your HANDS'"

"I held my hands up and he just smiled. There was not a mark on me, except for my hands, which were quite a mess from colliding with the other boy's faces. I never had much trouble anymore with people trying to pick on me, at least at school and I felt much more confident with myself."

Jack remained a good friend and I continued to help him with yard work. He was also there the day I left for the West Coast to train for the Navy. I never saw him again. He passed away before I would return, but I still do think of him and what he did to help me."

Chapter 14

- - -

My trip to the Navy and more about Isaac

My trip started as most would on a train. The first stop was New York City and to an induction center for medical testing. This is part of the induction process when you enlist. After passing the tests it was off to Penn Station and to the Great Lakes Naval Training Center. There is not much to say other than this was extremely hard work. They drilled you, toughened you up and got you ready to fight. Again Jack's work was helpful. What he made me do working in the yard and training helped me. If not for physical strength, in the way of dealing with performing mindless hard tasks. After 10 weeks of processing and work we were on a train again.

This time the train had open sides on some cars and hard wicker seats. The kind of wicker that leaves a print on your backside right through your pants, so you either have to sit on something, anything, or move around a lot. It was summer and hot so this helped keep you cooler, but comfort still eluded us.

I continued my story after a trip that seemed never to end we arrived in San Francisco to get our assignments.

Steven then said, " What about you Isaac how did you get to port, or for that matter how did you get involved with the apparel industry?"

Isaac said, " Well, that is quite a story, but also short and simple. I was on a train also. Not the same one as his, but his description for the most part is what we endured and the rest you already know.

When I left the Navy in the 1950's people were making efforts to give veterans jobs as part of retraining. I was contacted by a man who wanted me to work for him. He was an older guy, older than all of us actually. "

I had my chance to interrupt Isaac and did with pleasure I said, "Steven, it was different. Then you were hired because you knew how to do something. If you went to college, this was good, but you were wanted because of your work experience. Some guys would work for free, or very low wages as apprentices just to gain job experience."

Isaac jumped in interrupting me, " Yes, today is different. All they ask is where did you go to school. If you say I have master's in child psychology and good grades you have the job. A person who was raised well-adjusted, smart kids would not even be considered for the same job without the degree. I do not want to take anything away from education, but life experiences with success are much better markers. How many times did school teach you something and we find out 30 or 40 years later they were wrong. Well, you Steven, still have a few years to go."

Steven then said, " Not really, this has been an education in just the last few hours and I can see some things right now."

Isaac then continued with his original story," My first boss after the US Navy was not much of a businessman. We were often in a cash flow jam. He was very lucky though, at least I thought so. It was like a miracle how he would be able to pull us back from the brink of nothing using the stock market for unbelievable gains. That always fixed the situation and we would move on. Later as the years progressed I took over the business and we did not have such management issues, although I was never quite as *lucky* with the stock market as he was." Isaac made an unusual facial expression as he finished the phrase.

Steven then asked, " What happened to him?"

Issac said, "We lost touch over the years. He got involved with politics and was one of the last Presidents of the United States of America."

Steven was shocked, but did not probe any further. The fact that this man was so important at one time and Issac made light of knowing it was reason enough to change the subject.

Chapter 15

- - -

Chief Igor Brunsen

Then Isaac said, " You remember the chief don't you".

I leaned back and said with a sigh and said, "Yes."

I then said, "The chief took us both under his wing. Me for being a hardhead and Isaac for being different." Because we were so young, when we would put into port he would take us out into the town.

"Chief Brunsen was larger than life, overweight but, not by much and with a large red face. He had a voice and personality to match."

I then continued, " He would bark out orders always with a descriptive phase of you knuckleheads, little bastards, don't screw this one up, etc. He did not say it in a hurtful way, it was his manner. He watched over us more than the other guys. He knew I was much younger than I should be and Isaac just needed the watching."

Isaac then said, " Yeah, remember our first liberty in port."

I said, "Yes I do, I still have the scar, pointing to my forehead. "

Steve asked, "How did you do that?"

I said, " Well its part of a story, We have a few more minutes, We set into port in this small island that is basically a ship repair yard with a few bars. A real rough spot, but a favorite one because it is the last stop before the real fighting in the hot Pacific zone started. The commander of the boat would have the chief watch over the new guys, or the guys who just seemed to get into trouble. Isaac and I would probably just be happy staying on the boat and having no tasks to complete, but the commander would not have this. He said everyone deserves a night out, you never know when it may be your last."

I continued, "Chief Brunsen took us to one of his favorite spots, a bar and grill. We sat and drank and ate the meat of a stew that contained some kind of beast; we did not ask what it was, although it did not taste too bad."

I continued," We were not there too long until a fight broke out. The chief who was supposed to watch us took no time to get into the middle of it with guys from another boat, who pulled me and Isaac into it and shortly thereafter the military police showed up."

I continued, "The chief grabbed us and we headed for the bathroom where we quickly blocked the door."

Isaac piped in, " Yeah what a move that was, with heavy security screen on the one and only window. We were trapped like rats in a cage."

I then continued, " That did not stop the chief. He built up a head of steam, bent over and tore the toilet out of the floor, water and all. He then proceeded to run with it and threw it through the window, security screen and all. Out into the back street it went with all the window fixings. The people walking in the dark area got quite a surprise that night watching a toilet blast its way through the window and smash onto the street.

The chief then grabbed Isaac and threw him out the window."

Isaac then said, "You forgot the part where the chief missed and I bounced off the ceiling on the way out."

I said, "Yes I did, I also made sure I helped aim myself when it was my turn."

After we escaped, I said, " Let's get back to the boat."

The chief said, " Nothing doing, the night is still young and we have places to go."

I continued, "At the end of the night the Chief was carrying Isaac on his back and steering me down the street back to the boat. He had removed Isaac's glasses and put them in his shirt pocket, so Isaac would not lose them. After pausing to urinate on a building still holding Isaac on his back we continued. He was not steering very well as he walked me right into a light post and almost knocked my head off."

I continued. "The next morning at roll call we all lined up, I had a black eye and a bandage on my forehead, pointing to it. Isaac had no glasses, he could not see a thing. The chief looked all redfaced as he usually did every morning, like it was business as usual. The boat commander walked out to see what we looked like after our night of fun. He walked through the ranks of the men looking at scuffed up hands from fighting, faces that saw some action and then he paused at me. He saw my eye and head."

Then he commented, " I see the chief did a bang up job watching over you."

I continued, "The commander smiled a little, as he knew some of us would probably not be around in a short while and wanted to keep the morale up."

Isaac then said, " When the commander was occupied with someone else the chief slipped in back of me pulled my glasses out of his pocket and put them on my face roughly from behind me. The chief then said, thought you would need these. I was holding them for you last night, as he roughly tapped one of his knuckles on my head to emphasize the point, in his own way."

I continued, "We had a lot of good times with him. During ship time he was hard as usual, but after shift he was like a crazy uncle. Not having a family, he unofficially adopted us as his family and watched out for us. He would always say, knock it off or I'll send you both to the moon, making a fist gesture. That is until one day......"

Isaac and I both looked down, and Isaac continued, " We had a call to battle stations on the Washington. I was on the radar control gun and was having problems getting it to fire. We had issues with the control system."

Issac continued, "The chief in his usual manner carried a Tommy Gun, the kind gangsters used in the 1920's. He would shoot at the enemy planes with he was not at a normal battle station."

I said, "We were getting strafed by enemy planes. That is where they fly low and shoot at the ship. My position was out front with the radar gun and we were vulnerable. When the chief saw the gun malfunctioning he stood out front and fired on the planes with the Tommy gun. He hit two of them and then we did not hear the Tommy gun anymore. The chief must have been hit and fell over the side. All we found was his dog tags and the Tommy gun by the ship rail. The commander let me keep both of them, although I had to give the gun up years later. Even though it was an antique, the laws of the day did not allow a private citizen to own such a weapon. I turned it in as I was supposed to and it was destroyed."

I continued, "We were both transferred to the USS Missouri shortly after that. It was an Iowa class battleship. It was huge and was only dwarfed by the aircraft carriers that came into service. The ship had all the modern equipment of the day and we did well. I still missed the feeling of family we had with the chief on the Washington."

Chapter 16

- - -

The basement to freedom

We all got back into the van after our quick diversion in Isaac's hideout. The neighborhood looked much different, more in a state of renewal instead of decay. Isaac sat back he pushed back in the seat and then said, " I know where, but I can't take you all the way myself. There is an old tunnel you can use, that's as far as I can go."

I then said, "Where?"

Isaac said, "You will see".

We again sped through the streets with no regard for traffic control or speed. Only the sound of Isaac as he chuckled while he regularly exceeded the speed limit and violated numerous other traffic regulations. He was amused to see them build up on his PDA as if it did not matter.

He pulled in front of an abandoned building, he then handed me his PDA and said, "You will need this. In the basement is a sub-basement, which leads to another sub basement and an old service tunnel. Follow it and you will be where you need to be."

Steve and I got out of the van and just looked at him, " He then said I know, I know, you can never be too careful. I always like a few options in case the chips are down". Then he pointed to the building with haste.

The three of us quickly walked into the building then looked and eventually found the basement. Yes it was as you expected, disgusting, dirty and full of vermin, both the four-legged and two-legged kind.

Isaac said, "This is where I leave you both, be careful."

Steven and I traveled past pretty much unnoticed and I found the sub-basement, the next sub basement and finally a tunnel, Isaac's PDA screen lighting my way.

As I left the tunnel I received a text from Isaac, hastily done and again out of the ordinary. A guy who hates texting managed to send two in one day. That's probably more than he sends in a year. The text said "They know," hastily sent from a random number of one of his employee's pdas.

I exited the old building basement and noticed I was in the old 1964 Worlds Fair Grounds. The old rusting globe that was an icon of the day was a dead giveaway. We then found safety in an old recycling dumpster full of plastics while contemplating our next move.

Steven asked me, "Why did you send your daughter to the 1940's?"

I replied, "To keep her safe, so she can live out her life. She has an allergy to foods that they consider to be a burdening expense on the medical system, a genetic predisposition. As a result, when this is discovered in an individual you are given minimal care and god forbid if you ever need anything important medically, you will be only given comfort care. You are prohibited to get married and have children, so as to not possibly pass on the trait. You are just finished and they no longer have any use for you."

I continued, " You know how the national medical plan works, it is all free, they handle everything and all is well unless someone is ill. Then they decide on the best way to save cost. Even if you have money you can't buy services, this depletes the resources of available services.

Years ago this was set in motion. The services to the elderly were cut back to fund the needs of the young. It did not have to be this way. When insurance was private, services could be purchased and there was plenty of capacity for all. The powers that be at the time felt the system was not fair. I can admit it wasn't perfect, but so much more flexibility was available."

I continued, "One by one services were cut back and people were dying before their time. This is not frowned upon by the government. If you don't pay for their care you save money and when they are not around they save by not having to send those government checks out every month for retirement. I understand that if you save someone's life in their seventies you are only adding a five or ten years, but to that person and their family the five or ten years are precious. These are the grandparents and great-aunts and uncles who watch your kids while you are at work and help you raise them. If you take these people out of the equation by limiting their medical coverage you are taking them out of the raising of their grandchildren and the family connections are lost. They are raised by institutions when you can't be there. The result is un-caring and non-empathetic people, like we have today."

I continued, "If you have an elderly person in the family that needs care you should bring them into your home, then this is the standard. If you send them away to some cold utilitarian complex for care that becomes the standard. Don't be surprised if that is where you will end up if you need care someday, because you set the standard years ago. Kids are good learners of the good and the bad. They learn from example more than anything else. You don't need a master's degree in child psychology to know this, although I am sure there are some who have these credentials and think otherwise.

I continued, "You have to remember if it were not for my generation, you all would all be speaking German and

Japanese. You with your heritage, Steven, would probably not even be here at all."

I continued, "The only way my daughter could live out her life as it was intended to be was in the past. To be sure she was all right, I arranged it so that I could correspond with my earlier life. Even though I would not know it when we met at that time, but someday I would know she was all right because I saw it in the past and would become aware of it later. I would be able to spend some time with her also. Does this make sense?"

Steven said, "Totally".

Steve then said, " What was it like when we were a nation instead of just another state. "

I then said, "What do you mean?"

Steven said, " When we were a country instead of part of the World Order as a state?"

I then said, " Oh aren't we looking for trouble today. You know talking about that kind of thing will get you in a lot of trouble."

With that we both looked at each other and broke out into laughter, like we could be in any more trouble than we were already in now.

I looked at him and said, " You were free, but not truly free as freedom was dissolving over the years long before we succumb to becoming just a state instead of a nation. It all started with the powers that be looking over your shoulder. I was asleep like many people. If I had to do it all over again things would be different I promise you that."

I could see he understood and today he grew up a lot. I had done what Doug asked my to do, get him ready and I did. I got him ready for the company and everyone else.

Feeling my pocket I took out the small foil pouch. Wiggling it in between my figures I said to myself only in an emergency, well I guess this is an emergency.

I tore the small tattered foil pouch and proceeded to call the phone number listed at the top on Isaac's pda. A sharp voice answered hello. I proceeded to read a code on line 3 as instructed to do many years ago. After finishing there was silence. The voice now sounding more anxious and said, "Your phrase please."

As this is happening a senior government official somewhere else receives an urgent notice. He gets up and walks out of his meeting with the cabinet. Although generally not acceptable, all in the meeting knew the tone of the notice and knew not to ask any questions. They continued to meet as if the person were still in his chair.

As the message is read a profile came up. The profile reads a name of the cardholder and also a list of accomplishments, two of which catch his eye, gravitational propulsion and temporal realignment. Seeing this he made up his mind. He had seen the flash and how the cardholder, me, is wanted by the authorities and it all came together.

He slid a card similar to a credit card in a specialized reader and entered a code number, then pushed send and walked back into his meeting noticed, but unnoticed by all. This set off another event where by another more senior government official was alerted and followed a similar procedure.

Over 6,000 miles away a submerged automated spacecraft carrier races toward the surface of the ocean, bursting on to the surface of the water with a jolt and then settling to a perfectly smooth horizontal plane to the rough seas as the gravitational control system stabilizes the craft to the earth's gravitational field.

One of three elevators lifts out of its watertight cavities exposing an automated flat black craft ready for takeoff.

Still on the phone, he then repeats the phrase that was to go along with the card "Houston we have a problem". The voice then softens and says, "Well, it has been a long time since we heard from you, 28 years. Two more years and the government would have shut this system down as we were thinking there were none of you left."

I said, "Well at least something is working for me today. The voice then says based upon what I am reading half the nations private security are looking for you. Not very complimentary what they are charging you with, obviously wrong if they knew who you really were.

I responded, "I know."

A few years ago local police were replaced for the most part with private services. These services were not regionally based, but individual, or corporation based. Where ever the company operated the security forces were present. When you had a security issue you called your private force and they handled the issue and yes the company interest was the foremost goal.

Although some Cities still had municipal police forces, most were very small and traffic specific for the most part.

The voice on the phone continued, "We are obligated to help you, but you understand a few people will probably lose their lives just doing their job. Are you ready to deal with that?"

I think to my self before I answered, I wonder if she will really help me, or help me off the planet the hard way?

I then reply "Yes, it wouldn't be the first time."

The voice then says, "We will defend you against all pursuit you to prevent capture, even if it means ultimately your destruction."

I respond "I understand. "

The voice then asks. "Are you in an appropriate location?" " I responded you tell me",

With less than a chuckle, but with amusement the voice says, "Ok, good luck."

With that authorization code locked within the craft's computer it left the deck of the craft quickly accelerating with its own internal gravitational suppression systems straining to keep the power of the acceleration from tearing the crafts apart. These crafts bear no markings except where the American Flag and official markings were obscured beyond recognition by the patch coat of paint. It only bears the gold insignia of an ancient torch, the kind held by human for lighting one's way.

The craft skimming above the surface of the water quickly determined the best way to proceed and continued upward into the uppermost atmosphere and into a wide orbit, where it finished its acceleration and began its decent to the target, me.

As all this happens the private security forces amass in the area adjacent to the dumpster at the entrance to the park. I notice the pda shuts off on its own as if controlled by another force, the voice at the other end of the call goes silent. I peek out of a corner at the impending confusion and a second later there was a loud crash sending the dumpster hurdling into the air bouncing end over end.

This craft does not have bombs, or guns, it simply flew over their target at low altitude. It uses a plasmatic magnetic energy shield that allows it to travel through the Earth's atmosphere at over 500,000 knots, attack speed. At the target this unmanned drone releases its plasmatic magnetic shield of protection and in an instant the skin of the craft strikes and ignites the hydrogen in the atmosphere unleashing a localized blast that is devastating to any and all below.

We climbed out of the flipped over recycling dumpster and I discovered I had a dislocated shoulder. I pop my shoulder back in, and thought, that was not very pleasant and then looked out at the area in front of me. Rather than the former park it looked more like the face of the moon, caused by a blast set off by the craft. Nothing was recognizable.

I said to Steven, " Make your way back to the office. They are not looking for you and you maybe can blend in, if you change your torn clothes that is. Remember, you never saw me and they won't ask. You also have a new client

Isaac. He will buy from you and watch out for you. Do not tell anyone anything we told you. It is not to protect us, but more to protect you."

Steven agreed and we parted.

The only other thought that came through my head as I walked through the debris field was, **It really works.**

Chapter 17

- - -

The Ride Home

I make my way through the sea of people, all in their own world, speaking to others on the pdas while looking at you as they stare off. I know I should not travel home, but I am tired and have nowhere else to go. After stopping at a store to buy a new suit, I was moving again. I charged the suit to Isaac, well I had his pda and I'm sure he would have wanted it that way.

It is often hard to judge whether people are addressing you, or you just happen to be where they are looking. Everyone was talking about the freak lighting bolt or old space debris. Some were talking about a meteorite that possibly devastated the old World Fair Grounds.

The safest way to not be embarrassed by involving yourself into someone else's conversation is to wait for them to say it twice. If they say something twice while looking at you they are usually fair game for you to respond, and if you do you are usually right, or they violated protocol by looking at you too long while talking to someone else electronically.

Anyway, my seat is comfortable even with the imaginary square in my rear pocket that causes me to lean a little to the side. On the train car video monitor and through the clatter of others pdas is a story. No longer about me, but the meteorite that hit the park, or possibly a piece of space debris and the destruction it caused. As the train stopped a slim man got on, looked right at me and sat down.

He said in a hushed tone, "Please get off with me at the next stop." As we rode I saw the monitor on the train wall list all those killed or injured in the blast. As the names roll down I see a number of impossibilities. Since the blast took place miles from the building where we worked, or any building for that matter. I see Mikes name and the names of three others from the companies top management, also my own. I looked at the slim man and he looked at me and said, "They tempted the meteorite didn't they?"

It is as if the events of the past few hours did not exist and never happened. There was a news story and everyone accepted it as the actual events and that was it.

Now there was no doubt in my mind this man was associated with the voice on the phone. The train begins to slow.

On the other side of the seat a little boy is sitting holding an old tattered book. . The book must belong to his parents, as no one buys paper books anymore. Everything is electronic and easy, easy for companies to see what you like to read. He must be learning to read as he stumbles. He keeps saying, "on u a tim… once upn a tim…"

I keep saying to my self come on you can do it, spit out and read me the rest of it, the impatient side of me popping out for a minute. He was conscious that I was looking at him and knew I was waiting for him to say it. Then he finally says it " Once Upon a Time and he stops and looks at me. I then fill in the rest by thinking it, but it actually came out of my mouth in a little more than a whisper, "we were free".

A few people within a close earshot look up for a brief moment as if someone were to overhear someone saying free coffee today at Tenbucks. They soon fell back into what had their attention to begin with as the train motion and noise stopped and fell silent. The slim man looks at me then smiles as we exit the train.

As I step out on to the platform I see my wife standing there with another gentleman. In her hand a small suitcase with a few items that were hastily packed.

As I walked up she commented to me, " I thought you were going to behave yourself today?"

I looked at her and then shrugged my shoulders a little.

The second man began to speak, "We have to relocate you both, this time new names for identification. Not that

I can accommodate you anywhere, but we will take it into consideration."

I stood there and thought about it. Then I said, " 1942 and there will be three of us traveling also."

With this my wife took my hand and squeezed it tight with approval. The man looked a little angry and said, " You, messing with temporal physics again."

I said, " Yes, but this will correct an imbalance, we will all be together now, just in a different time."

As I said that, I looked up at the flagpole again. Although I saw the World Order flag with its black field and symbol of a torch on it when we exited the train, someone must have changed it when we were not looking, but this was impossible. I would have seen them. It is as if the old flag was not there and it was replaced of all things with the American flag. I had not seen that flying for quite some time because it was illegal.

With that the old gentleman thought about my request for three to travel and with an indifferent expression on his face nodded a little. As he did a car pulled up for our ride. Out of the vehicle four people exited.

Two were wearing black suits, obviously they were security oriented, one was a lady with a leather folder and much younger and another was a gentleman who was quite old, but familiar. Clearly these people were the staff of the older gentleman, although the lady called the gentleman great grand pop once by accident.

We walked off the platform and toward the vehicle. There was something about the old gentleman that was familiar, yet different.

As we walked up the two security staff had a look of surprise and delight on their faces, the kind when you meet someone who is a celebrity. I looked at them and said, "Well you're both in a good mood today."

They said, "Yep and we are here to escort you on your journey to the 1940's." I was taken back by this statement because I had just stated this intention before they arrived and they had no way of knowing it.

The lady stepped forward and responded, "Pleased to meet you, sir."

I took her hand in a gentle shake and responded, "Charmed to meet you also."

The older gentleman walked from in back of the security staff and as he did one of the staff took his hand to steady him and said "Here let me help you, Mr. President."

Obviously, he was not the president now, but still important and under the watchful eye of the government for his safety.

As he looked up at me it became clear. He was I and it looks like I kept my word to Steven.

We all got into the car and I sat there for a moment thinking about what to say to myself (him) or what to ask. Then I started speaking to him (my older self that is) and said, " I want to be careful what I tell you so I will only repeat what you told me some time ago, at least the older you, me, well you know what I mean right?"

Before I could even answer my older self started talking again. Truly he was me, he continued, "When I was making the same journey you are about to make. This is what I was told. Let's stay on what worked in the past and not create any variables."

He continued, "We are not part of the World Order, at least as a state. We are our own country, see the flag up there, " as he pointed to the station flag pole." I nodded.

He then continued, " Everything you remember about the dumpster and the explosion did not happen. You may remember it as if it did, but that is only because you are part of the temporal change. Those directly involved in changing events remember the old and the new as it happens in the future, but not as it happened in the past as a result of the change. That is why you remember everything as it was and not as it is now. It is very important that you keep this in mind."

He continued, "You ran for Congress and then later the Senate. You won both seats. Well only one at first and it took two tries for the second. You also won the highest office, well you already knew that."

Now I am a little perplexed, but trying to grasp this all.

He continued, " You do not work for the company, you work for the State Department now.

He continued, "You stopped the separate treatment of subclasses of citizens, unless reviewed on an individual basis. "

He continued, " The legal alcohol limit nationwide for driving over the limit is .0125, applied equally against all citizens, unless on an individual basis there is reason for you to be held to a lower, or none at all in your system, or for medical reasons. Special interest groups get no special treatment for that would take advantage of the government and the individual person."

He continued, " One person one vote and you need a State or national issued I.D to vote and full citizenship. The elections are truly secret ballots calculated by electro mechanical voting machines that prevent fraud. No paper ballots are allowed where fingerprints or DNA can be lifted from the ballot pages. With paper, people can try to determine who a person voted for."

Then he said finally, " Now is time for your favorite parts," as he sat forward and smiled.

He then said, " No social organization, media company or application can track, record, picture match, use, list or sell any personal data. They can sell products to you and market you for services, but that is it. If they are to retain any information regarding you or your habits then they must upon each instance of use, get your specific permission to do so. This is done without any implications to limit your use to less than someone who allows this tracking or use. Employers and government have no place in your social media' or any right to review this information."

He continued, "The government can be involved if you plan to commit an illegal act using the service. If you accept someone in a supervisory role to view your information, or they happen to view your personal page, they cannot use anything posted on your personal account for employment purposes without your permission. You are prohibited to provide permission for anything that will be used for a purpose that is not in your personal best interest."

I sat back in my seat feeling quiet impressed with myself or at least him, my older self, I know what I mean, I think.

I then said, " How did we get these items passed?"

My older self said, "It was so easy in the 1960's and 1970's. We just tagged it on to the other laws and policies being approved. People did not even know what we were talking about, although a few did comment that I, you ah we, were crazy why even list the impossible, but they humored us and we passed it anyway."

As we drove he then pointed out the window to a large ship flying across the sky. He said, "We were responsible for that also, the Enterprise, a museum piece today but still very important. It is being flown to Houston for an air and space show. We have been to the moon, Mars, the outer planets and that ship has been to Alpha Centauri, the closest star and back.

My older self then said, " I have the chief's Tommy gun"

I replied, "How did you manage that, I had to give that weapon up years ago."

My older self then smiled and said, "No you didn't. You can have it back, if you like. I enjoyed it for years now it's your turn. Its amazing what you can do when you don't get bogged down in bullshit and focus on the problems for solutions, instead of the results of the problems."

Chapter 18

- - -

Responsibility and Justice

My older self then said, " Oh and by the way we were responsible for a few other things you should know about."

As he spoke I just envisioned what was being said, as it was a bit shocking.

I saw a guy working in a welding shop being approached by a government official. He was asked to come back and perform a very special task. He was to search for an individual that not many people heard of.

He an another searched the desert and other likely and unlikely areas of the world until one day he came across some information that lead him into the mountains of Afghanistan, a group of people in a planning meeting in a boarder town of Afghanistan. They got out of their vehicles in a mountainous terrain and enter a cave retreat in the side of a hill. One man was very tall and had a beard.

The team leader called this in on his communication device and also uploaded the long-range pictures for verification. It was a match.

At the same time I saw a hand going on a scanner screen of a small mobile device and a code being entering into a keypad. After entry a message lights up on the screen that said message received and authorized.

All this was taking place as the two men sat in their mountainous perch and waited. They had submitted the information they were supposed to and asked if they should wait for target verification, thinking this would be a normal air strike.

No one had gotten back to them and there they sat. The team leader knows a senior individual deployed in the Indian Ocean on a ship. This senior individual was a large redfaced man who often commented how things used to be different.

The team leader used his satellite phone and dialed this person. The redfaced man answered the his own satellite phone abruptly with a horse raspy voice and said, "I can't talk right now, we have problems here."

The person in Afghanistan then said, " What's going on?"

The person aboard ship said, "I don't know."

Then he said more than he should, as he knew the information maybe useful to his friend.

The redfaced man held the phone away from his face and barked directions at his staff, "We are rigging for a major EMP (electromagnetic pulse) here, hurry up shutting down all equipment on board. We need to protect it from the effects."

The large redfaced man returned the phone to his face and the man in Afghanistan said " Well I'll leave you to this. Thank you." then hung up.

He then looked at his partner on the mission and said, "This is not going well."

In a desolate area of North Dakota in a large open wild field the peace is disturbed by a loud metallic banging noise and the whoosh of a small rocket mechanism that is activated to slide a huge metal door about 30 feet. There is quiet again for a few seconds just to be disrupted by a thunderous roar of a rocket engine that pushes its craft at first slowly and then with greater speed as it leaves its silo. A skyward view of the ground shows that although only one lifts toward space, this is only one of potentially many that still sit dormant. This device built over 35 years earlier is now hurling skyward.

At the same time a phone that normally does not ring begins to chime. This phone is located in the Russian Federations Strategic Defense Ministry.

As the phone is lifted with hesitancy the person says "ЗраВсТВуите" which is pronounced zdrah.stu.it.eh and would be translated as hello in English. The voice on the other end of the phone acknowledges and says, "You see something don't you."

The person who answers the phone sheepishly says "yes".

The voice then said, "You know this is not meant for you." There is silence for a moment.

The voice then said, "If it were meant for you they all would be on their way, right?"

The person who answered the phone remains silent for a moment then says, "Then where is it going?"

The voice then said, "Somewhere that should please you, you will see, it will be alright."

The voice then said, "So are we alright?"

The person who answered the phone then said, "I guess we are if what you say is true."

The voice then said, "Very good"and hung up.

The man in Afghanistan has a problem. If he tries to leave he will be spotted and if he can get away so can his target. He sits and waits and then confides in his partner.

His partner was much younger and clearly was willing to do almost anything for his government, but getting blown up by a nuclear weapon was not one of those things. He is clearly losing his edge and potentially will compromise the mission. This man is thinking of his wife and his small children and it is not going well.

The team leader then said. "Let's try and leave I will approach the group of guards on the other side of the hill. You come around and help when the time comes." With that he adorns his head with a robe and tried to look like he is traveling in the desert.

He leaves his perch undetected until his performance begins in one of the native languages of Dari.

He says, as he stumbles and approaches the three rear guards as they immediately take up arms, " سلام آقا خوب من در صحرا گم شده" Translated as, Hello fine sir I am lost in the desert.

The guards still alerted look at him a little softer. The man then approaches closer and says, "Can you help me find my way."

Now in the kill zone he pulls out his piston and takes the first guard out as he ducks behind a rock. His partner now undetected in the crossfire zone has an easy shot and finishes the other two guards.

With that the two men jump into a rugged vehicle that looks more like an armed car and speeds away down a long straight road as fast as they can as the turbo diesel engine grinds to full operating speed leaving a large cloud of black dirty smoke.

The team leader says, "This may work out better." The enemy will be drawn into the open, although the cave will offer little in the way of cover for the blast that is coming.

His partner says, "Will we make it?"

The team leader says, I don't know, as he looks around the back of the car while driving. He then says, seeing curtains to shield the rear windows from the sun, " Close all those curtains and break the rear view mirror on the outside of the vehicle. You don't want the flash of light to blind you, if it catches you wrong."

His partner quickly complies breaking both rear view mirrors he could reach and closes the curtains. At the same time the team leader smashes the mirror on the drivers door as they approach the crest of a rise now a good distance from their original location.

After a short flight there is a bright flash and a region of this mountain range of Afghanistan became uninhabitable for a few thousand years.

The team leader and his partner are aware of this as the curtains in back of the vehicle start to smolder from the bright blast of heat. At the same time the vehicles steering begins to lock and looses responsiveness and the brakes just shutdown and become inoperable also. The brakes' malfunction was unnoticed at first because all the electronic equipment on the dashboard begins to smoke and pass small lightning bolts between them and the men just hold their hands and feet in the air to avoid being in contact with the shocks.

This condition is shortlived as the force of the blast catches up with them and they in their armored vehicle are hurled into the air, coming to a rather abrupt landing in a pile of sand and rocks.

The team leader who was sitting with his eyes shut opens one eye to the amazement that they are still alive. The diesel engine still running, until his partner says the engine is still running. Right at that point the engine turns its last and stops.

As that part of the story ends I then pressed back in my seat and said, "That must not have gone to well, did it with the world, the American people?"

My old self said, "No it did not. It was the end of my first term, so I got off easy with just not being re-elected."

He also continued, " It could have been much worse, jail time, who knows, but it was alright especially when the world did some investigating and found out who was at the meeting and the laws that govern this type of action."

I then said, "Was it worth it?"

My older self said, "Worth, it is a relative term, I knew I was changing the future, but no one else did because this was still their first time through, their only time with nothing to compare it to. Only one thing kept me safe. Something I put into a law in the 1960's. It was a law that said the executive branch could take action to ensure the temporal time line heads in a direction that will uphold the basic principals of the Constitution and safety of the American people. Not many elected officials who voted on it understood what was meant by this nor did they care. It was a small part of something very much bigger that a number of them wanted and needed. It remained hidden for years, until I needed it. This law did give me the option to do what I did and it was the break I needed, The unknown factor of what could have been and that was enough for me to get away with it."

We were traveling on the New Jersey turnpike in the area of Fort Lee. I always liked to gaze upon New York City and see Freedom Tower towering above the skyline from here, as it is quite a nice view of the city. I had been preoccupied with the conversation and did not notice where we were.

I shrugged and said, " What were you changing? "

My older self, Mr. Ex-President, pointed out the window and then I knew. The view of the city was not what I expected. Where there was one, currently, or a least what I expected to be my current day there were two. Two shining tall towers that were still remembered in the time I remember, but not often talked about, still standing where they were built some 70 years earlier.

I looked up and nodded my approval.

My older self then said, " And they who were saved put up the biggest stink about what I did. The ones who were saved made the biggest fuss over the whole issue, not knowing or even believing what I had done ultimately saved them."

I look at him smiled and said, " Why should that day be any different?"

We both chucked getting our joke and understanding that you cannot please everyone, even those whom you saved from certain destruction.

The end

www.ingramcontent.com/pod-product-compliance
Lightning Source LLC
Chambersburg PA
CBHW072007170626
46813CB00005B/2049